PERCY JACKSON & THE OLYMPIANS

BOOK FOUR

THE BATTLE OF THE LABYRINTH

The Graphic Novel

by

RICK RIORDAN

Adapted by
Robert Venditti

Art by
Orpheus Collar
and **Antoine Dodé**

Lettering by
Chris Dickey

DISNEP · HYPERION
Los Angeles New York

Adapted from the novel
Percy Jackson & the Olympians, Book Four: *The Battle of the Labyrinth*

First Edition, October 2018
1 3 5 7 9 10 8 6 4 2
FAC-008598-18236
Printed in the United States of America

This book is set in Adobe Caslon Pro/Adobe;
MonsterFonts-HouseofTerror, Tiki-Island/House Industries

Layouts and Color by Orpheus Collar
Pencils and Inks by Antoine Dodé
Designed by Jim Titus

Library of Congress Cataloging-in-Publication Data

Names: Venditti, Robert, author. • Riordan, Rick. Battle of the Labyrinth.
Title: The battle of the Labyrinth : the graphic novel / by Rick Riordan ; adapted by Robert Venditti ;
art and color by Orpheus Collar and Antoine Dode.
Description: First graphic novel edition. • Los Angeles ; New York : Disney-Hyperion, 2018. • Series:
Percy Jackson & the Olympians ; book 4 • Summary: When demonic cheerleaders invade his high school, Percy
Jackson hurries to Camp Half-Blood, from whence he and his demigod friends set out on a quest through the
Labyrinth, while the war between the Olympians and the evil Titan lord Kronos draws near.
Identifiers: LCCN 2017053599 • ISBN 9781484782354 (hardcover) • ISBN 9781484786390 (paperback)
Subjects: LCSH: Graphic novels. • CYAC: Graphic novels. • Mythology, Greek—Fiction. • Labyrinths—
Fiction. • Camps—Fiction. • Monsters—Fiction. • Animals, Mythical—Fiction. • Titans (Mythology)—
Fiction. • Riordan, Rick. Battle of the Labyrinth—Adaptations.
Classification: LCC PZ7.7.V48 Bat 2018 • DDC 741.5/973—dc23
LC record available at https://lccn.loc.gov/2017053599

ISBN (hardcover) 978-1-4847-8235-4
ISBN (paperback) 978-1-4847-8639-0

Reinforced binding

Follow @ReadRiordan and visit www.DisneyBooks.com

NEW YORK CITY.

GYMNASIUM

NINTH GRADE ORIENTATION DAY.

RUN!

LET ME GO!

BAND ROOM

WHAT THE *HECK* IS THE MATTER WITH YOU?

I SHOW UP FOR MY *FIRST DAY* AT A NEW SCHOOL, AND YOU GO *NUTS!*

ARE THEY FOLLOWING US?

IS *WHO* FOLLOWING US? WHAT'RE YOU *TALKING* ABOUT?

WHO ARE YOU?

BE QUIET!

WAIT... I REMEMBER YOU. HOOVER DAM, RIGHT?

YOUR NAME IS RACHEL. *RACHEL ELIZABETH DARE.* WHAT ARE YOU DOING IN NEW YORK?

I REMEMBER YOU ALMOST GOT ME *KILLED.* YOU HAD A PEN, BUT IT WAS A *SWORD.* AND THERE WERE COPS CHASING YOU, BUT THEY WERE *ZOMBIES.*

THEN I SEE YOU AT MY NEW SCHOOL-- AND I SEE *THEM*-- AND I'M, LIKE, *"HERE WE GO AGAIN."*

WHAT? WHAT DID YOU SEE?

JUST...NEVER MIND. YOU WON'T BELIEVE ME. I'M CRAZY, ALL RIGHT? THAT'S WHAT EVERYONE SAYS. I'M *CRAZY.*

RACHEL! YOU KNEW MY PEN WAS A SWORD. YOU KNEW THOSE COPS WEREN'T REALLY COPS.

IF YOU CAN SEE THROUGH THE *MIST,* I NEED TO KNOW WHAT YOU'RE RUNNING FROM.

AND I NEED TO KNOW *NOW.*

WHAT ARE YOU TALKING ABOUT? WHAT *"MIST"*?

IT'S...WELL, IT'S LIKE THIS VEIL THAT HIDES THE WAY THINGS REALLY ARE. SOME *MORTALS* ARE BORN WITH THE ABILITY TO SEE THROUGH IT. LIKE YOU.

MORTAL? YOU SAY THAT LIKE YOU'RE... *NOT.*

YOU KNOW WHAT IT ALL MEANS, DON'T YOU. ALL THESE *HORRIBLE* THINGS I SEE.

TELL ME. PLEASE.

LOOK, THIS IS GOING TO SOUND WEIRD. ALL THE GREEK MYTHS-- *GODS* AND *MONSTERS* AND *HEROES.*

THEY'RE *REAL.*

I *KNEW* IT! FOR YEARS I THOUGHT I WAS GOING *NUTS!* YOU HAVE NO IDEA HOW HARD IT'S BEEN.

OH, I THINK I HAVE A PRETTY GOOD IDEA.

SO WHO ARE YOU?

WHO ARE YOU *REALLY*?

MY NAME IS PERCY JACKSON. I'M A *HALF-BLOOD.*

I'M HALF HUMAN AND HALF...

THERE YOU ARE, PERCY JACKSON.

THOSE *KILLER CHEERLEADERS* DIDN'T WANT ME.

THEY'RE AFTER YOU.

YOU'D BETTER GET GOING.

SO, LIKE, ARE YOU GOING TO ALMOST GET ME KILLED *EVERY* TIME I SEE YOU?

POSSIBLY.

WELCOME TO *MY* WORLD.

MY PHONE NUMBER. I WANT TO KNOW MORE ABOUT HALF-BLOODS. AND GODS AND MONSTERS.

YOU *WILL* CALL ME.

YOU OWE ME THAT MUCH.

WAIT! DO YOU EVEN HAVE A *SAFE PLACE* TO GO?

A *SAFE PLACE*?

SOUNDS LIKE YOUR SUMMER STARTED WITH A *BANG*, SEAWEED BRAIN.

DON'T YOU USUALLY WAIT FOR A SCHOOL YEAR TO *START* BEFORE YOU DESTROY EVERYTHING?

ORIENTATION DAY HAS TO BE SOME KIND OF *HALF-BLOOD RECORD.*

YOU SOUND LIKE MY *MOM.*

SHE'S TAKING THIS ONE A LITTLE HARD, GOODE BEING WHERE HER BOYFRIEND, PAUL, TEACHES AND ALL.

HOW ABOUT YOU, ANNABETH?

HOW WAS EIGHTH GRADE?

MONSTER-INFESTED. THINGS ARE DEFINITELY GETTING *WORSE* OUT THERE.

IT'S GOOD TO BE BACK AT CAMP, I'LL SAY THAT.

ANY WORD ON *LUKE?*

MOUNT TAM IS STILL OVERRUN WITH MONSTERS.

I HAVEN'T BEEN BACK SINCE WE FOUGHT LUKE THERE LAST SUMMER.

BUT I DON'T THINK HE'S UP THERE. I THINK I'D KNOW IF HE WAS.

ANYWAY, YOU'VE GOT LOTS OF CATCHING UP TO DO.

COME ON.

"YOU NEED TO MEET THE NEW INSTRUCTOR."

MRS. O'LEARY! DOWN!

DON'T WORRY ABOUT HER, PERCY.

SHE'S HARMLESS, AS FAR AS HELLHOUNDS GO.

HARMLESS. RIGHT.

GRRRRRR

SHLORRRP

I'M QUINTUS. I'M HELPING OUT AT CAMP WHILE MR. D IS AWAY SHORING UP ALLIANCES.

AND YOU MUST BE PERCY JACKSON. ANNABETH HAS TOLD ME ALL ABOUT YOU.

I HEAR YOU'RE HANDY WITH A SWORD. I BELIEVE I'D LIKE TO SEE THAT.

WHAT'S IN THE CRATES, QUINTUS?

BAROOOOOOO

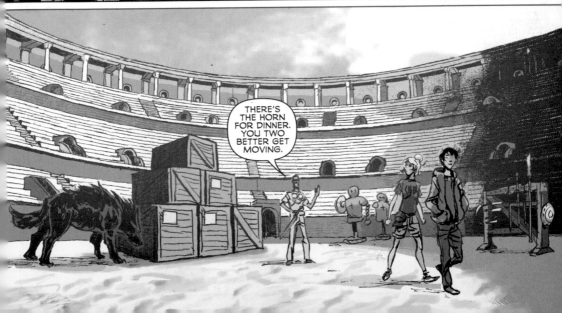

THERE'S THE HORN FOR DINNER. YOU TWO BETTER GET MOVING.

BROTHER! YOU'RE HERE!

NOW WE CAN EAT PEANUT BUTTER SANDWICHES AND RIDE *FISH PONIES* AND MAKE MONSTERS GO *BOOM!*

TYSON!

OW, WATCH THE RIBS. THE *RIBS*.

GROVER? NO SMILES? YOU'RE SEEING YOUR *BEST FRIEND* FOR THE FIRST TIME SINCE LAST SUMMER.

I'M SORRY, PERCY. IT'S JUST...

THE FAT *SATYR BOSSES* SAY GROVER IS A *LIAR*.

I TOLD THE *COUNCIL OF CLOVEN ELDERS* HOW I HEARD THE VOICE OF THE NATURE GOD *PAN* SPEAK TO ME DURING OUR QUEST LAST SUMMER, BUT THEY DON'T BELIEVE ME.

THEY SAID I ONLY HAVE ONE WEEK LEFT TO FIND PAN, OR THEY'RE GOING TO REVOKE MY *SEARCHER'S LICENSE* FOR GOOD.

I'LL BE A *DISGRACE* TO THE UNDERWOOD NAME.

MY DAD WAS A SEARCHER. MY GRANDFATHER WAS A SEARCHER...

HEY, DON'T WORRY. I'M HERE TO HELP. WE'LL FIGURE IT OUT.

ANNABETH AND CLARISSE THINK THEY MIGHT HAVE A PLAN...BUT THEY SAID IT'S DANGEROUS.

ANNABETH IS HANGING OUT WITH *CLARISSE*? THE SAME CLARISSE WHO TRIES TO *KILL* ME EVERY TIME SHE SEES ME?

WHAT CAN I SAY? TIMES ARE TOUGH AROUND HERE.

EVERYONE IS STRESSED OUT, WAITING FOR LUKE TO SHOW UP AND ATTACK AGAIN.

FATHER POSEIDON SAYS I SHOULD STAY HERE AND HELP MAKE WEAPONS. I WANTED TO STAY WITH HIM.

THE OLD *SEA MONSTERS* ARE GOING TO MAKE WAR ON HIM.

EVEN *DIONYSUS* FINALLY GOT OFF HIS LAZY REAR END.

ZEUS CALLED HIM BACK TO OLYMPUS TO HELP MAKE SURE ALL THE GODS AND MINOR GODS ARE LINING UP ON THE RIGHT SIDE.

THE WAR AGAINST *KRONOS* AND THE *TITANS* IS COMING, PERCY. I CAN FEEL IT.

PERCY?

"--PERCY JACKSON."

PERCY?

HM?

ARE YOU ALL RIGHT? DID YOU LISTEN TO ANYTHING I SAID?

YEAH, SORRY. I GUESS I'M JUST TIRED.

IT'S BEEN A LONG DAY FULL OF *HELLHOUNDS* AND *EXPLODING CHEERLEADERS.*

WELL, *SNAP* OUT OF IT.

WE HAVE TO MEET WITH ANNABETH AND CLARISSE TO DISCUSS PLANS.

NOT TONIGHT. I WON'T BE ANY GOOD.

TOMORROW, OKAY?

OKAY...

THE NEXT MORNING.

KNOCK KNOCK.

≶YAWN≷

ALL RIGHT! *ALL RIGHT!*

CHIRON? WHAT'S GOING ON?

I'LL LEAVE YOU TO DISCUSS THAT WITH YOUR FRIENDS.

WHERE'S TYSON?

HE LEFT EARLY FOR WEAPONS-FORGING CLASS. WHAT'S THIS ABOUT?

IT'S ABOUT THE *LABYRINTH.*

GROAN

LOOK, GROVER IS IN TROUBLE. THERE'S ONLY *ONE WAY* I CAN FIGURE TO HELP HIM. IT'S THE LABYRINTH. THAT'S WHAT CLARISSE AND I HAVE BEEN UP TO.

YOU MEAN THE MAZE FROM ANCIENT GREEK MYTHOLOGY? THE PLACE WHERE THEY KEPT THE MINOTAUR?

EXACTLY. IT MOVED TO THE UNITED STATES WITH THE HEART OF WESTERN CIVILIZATION, JUST LIKE MOUNT OLYMPUS BEING ABOVE THE EMPIRE STATE BUILDING.

EXCEPT THE LABYRINTH IS *HUGE.* IT KEPT GROWING OVER THE MILLENNIA. IT WOULDN'T FIT UNDER A SINGLE *CITY* ANYMORE, MUCH LESS A BUILDING.

SUPPOSEDLY, YOU CAN GET ANYWHERE THROUGH THE LABYRINTH. IF YOU DON'T GET *LOST.* OR DIE A *HORRIBLE DEATH.*

THERE HAS TO BE A WAY. CLARISSE SURVIVED. SO DID CHRIS.

HE ONLY GOT DRIVEN *INSANE.* THAT'S MUCH BETTER.

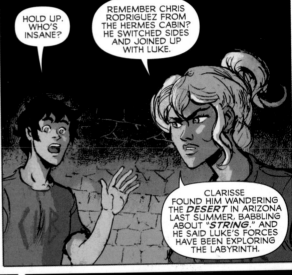

HOLD UP. WHO'S INSANE?

REMEMBER CHRIS RODRIGUEZ FROM THE HERMES CABIN? HE SWITCHED SIDES AND JOINED UP WITH LUKE.

CLARISSE FOUND HIM WANDERING THE *DESERT* IN ARIZONA LAST SUMMER, BABBLING ABOUT *"STRING."* AND HE SAID LUKE'S FORCES HAVE BEEN EXPLORING THE LABYRINTH.

AND...

YOU'RE *HOPELESS,* SEAWEED BRAIN.

THANK THE GODS *ONE* OF US IS A CHILD OF THE GODDESS OF WISDOM AND BATTLE STRATEGY.

COME ON, GRAB YOUR STUFF. WE'LL TALK MORE IN THE WOODS.

WHY ARE WE GOING TO THE WOODS?

QUINTUS ANNOUNCED *WAR GAMES.* YOU AND I HAVE BEEN PARTNERED UP.

"YOU COULD *DEFINITELY* USE THE TRAINING."

YOU ALL KNOW YOUR TWO-PERSON TEAMS.

YOUR GOAL IS SIMPLE: COLLECT THE *GOLD LAURELS* WITHOUT DYING.

THERE ARE SIX MONSTERS. EACH HAS A SILK PACKAGE TIED TO ITS BACK, BUT ONLY ONE HOLDS THE PRIZE.

YOU MUST FIND THE WREATH BEFORE THE OTHER TEAMS.

AND, OF COURSE, YOU'LL HAVE TO *SLAY* THE MONSTERS TO GET IT.

LET THE GAMES BEGIN!

YOU THINK GROVER AND TYSON WILL BE ALL RIGHT?

THEY'LL BE FINE. COME ON.

LET'S WORRY ABOUT HOW WE'RE GOING TO STAY *ALIVE*.

THE WOODS.

SO...*STRING*. WHAT DO YOU THINK CHRIS RODRIGUEZ WAS TALKING ABOUT?

IT HAS TO BE *ARIADNE'S STRING*. IT'S A MAGIC ITEM THAT HELPED THESEUS ESCAPE THE LABYRINTH IN THE OLD DAYS.

IF LUKE FINDS IT, HE'LL BE ABLE TO NAVIGATE THE LABYRINTH, MOVE HIS ARMY AROUND IN SECRET, AND *AMBUSH* ANYWHERE, ANYTIME.

MAYBE EVEN WITHIN THE BORDERS OF CAMP.

THE CLOSEST ENTRANCE CLARISSE FOUND WAS IN MANHATTAN. BUT THAT DOESN'T MEAN THERE AREN'T OTHERS.

ANNABETH... I HAD A VISION. I SAW *NICO DI ANGELO*. I THINK HE WAS IN THE UNDERWORLD. HE WAS WITH A GHOST. THEY'RE PLOTTING REVENGE AGAINST ME.

THE GHOST SAID SOMETHING ABOUT A *MAZE*.

THAT SETTLES IT. WE *HAVE* TO FIGURE OUT THE LABYRINTH.

WHATEVER COMES OUT OF THOSE BUSHES, I'LL DRAW ITS ATTENTION FORWARD. USE YOUR MAGIC HAT TO TURN INVISIBLE AND SNEAK AROUND BEHIND IT.

UM, PERCY?

RSSTL RSSTL

SHH! SOMETHING'S COMING!

UFF!

WMMMP

WHAT... WHERE ARE WE?

...IT'S A *CORRIDOR*.

PERCY, *DON'T MOVE*. WE NEED TO FIND THE EXIT. *NOW.*

WHAT DO YOU MEAN? IT'S RIGHT ABOVE--

...HOW?

WHERE'S THE OPENING WE FELL THROUGH?

THE *WALLS*, PERCY. HELP ME LOOK.

THANK THE GODS.

WHAT'S THAT?

THE MARK OF *DAEDALUS*.

CREEEEEAK

THIS IS CRAZY. WHAT WERE WE GONE, *FIVE MINUTES?* HOW IS IT NIGHT? WHAT HAPPENED TO THE SCORPIONS?

WE FOUND IT. I CAN'T BELIEVE WE FOUND IT.

WHAT, ANNABETH? *WHAT* DID WE FIND?

AN *INVASION ROUTE* STRAIGHT INTO THE HEART OF CAMP.

WE FOUND AN *ENTRANCE* TO THE *LABYRINTH*.

EXACTLY, CLARISSE, DAEDALUS IS THE GREATEST ARCHITECT AND INVENTOR OF ALL TIME. HE *BUILT* THE LABYRINTH. IF LUKE CONVINCES DAEDALUS TO HELP HIM, HE WON'T HAVE TO WORRY ABOUT TRAPS OR GETTING LOST.

DAEDALUS LIVED, WHAT, *THREE THOUSAND* YEARS AGO? ISN'T HE DEAD?

NO ONE KNOWS, QUINTUS. THERE ARE MANY *DISTURBING* RUMORS ABOUT DAEDALUS.

IF HE DISAPPEARED BACK INTO THE LABYRINTH, HE MAY YET BE ALIVE.

TIME IS SAID TO WORK *DIFFERENTLY* DOWN THERE.

HE COULD TAKE HIS ARMY ANYWHERE. FIRST TO CAMP TO DESTROY US. AND THEN... *OLYMPUS*.

WE HAVE TO FIND DAEDALUS FIRST. IF HE'S ALIVE, WE CONVINCE HIM TO HELP *US*, NOT LUKE.

AND IF ARIADNE'S STRING STILL EXISTS, WE MAKE SURE IT *NEVER* FALLS INTO LUKE'S HANDS.

WE NEED A *QUEST*. AND WE ALL KNOW WHO SHOULD LEAD IT.

ANNABETH.

NO WAY! THE PLACE IS A *DEATH TRAP!*

I'M OUR BEST CHANCE, PERCY. I'VE STUDIED THE LABYRINTH.

IN *BOOKS!* IT'S *NOT* THE SAME THING!

ENOUGH.

I DO NOT RELISH THE THOUGHT, BUT ANNABETH IS *BEST QUALIFIED* FOR THIS QUEST.

IF THERE ARE NO OBJECTIONS?

VERY WELL.

ANNABETH, IT'S YOUR TIME TO VISIT THE *ORACLE*. THEN WE SHALL DISCUSS WHAT TO DO NEXT.

"TOMORROW AT DAWN, WE SEND YOU INTO THE *LABYRINTH*."

ANNABETH? YOU OKAY?

I'VE WANTED TO LEAD A QUEST SINCE I WAS SEVEN.

I'M WORRIED, PERCY.

MAYBE I SHOULDN'T HAVE ASKED YOU TO DO THIS. OR TYSON AND GROVER.

HEY, IT'S... IT'S OKAY. WE'VE HAD PLENTY OF PROBLEMS BEFORE, AND WE SOLVED THEM.

I'VE NEVER SEEN YOU SO SCARED.

THIS IS *DIFFERENT*. I'M BREAKING THE RULES. BUT I DON'T KNOW WHAT ELSE TO DO. I NEED YOU THREE. IT JUST FEELS RIGHT.

IS THIS ABOUT THE *PROPHECY*? THE LAST LINE-- ABOUT A HERO'S LAST BREATH...

IS THERE ANOTHER LINE YOU'RE NOT TELLING US? THEY USUALLY RHYME. DOES IT END IN THE WORD...*DEATH*?

GO GET READY FOR THE QUEST, PERCY.

I'LL SEE YOU IN THE MORNING.

"WE AWAIT ONE FINAL HEART."

A GRAVEYARD.

THERE IS NO NEED SUMMON THE DEAD, NICO. YOU ALREADY HAVE ME FOR ADVICE.

I WANT A SECOND OPINION.

WHO ARE YOU, YOUNG WARRIOR? SPEAK.

I AM THESEUS.

HOW CAN I RETRIEVE MY SISTER?

DO NOT TRY. IT IS MADNESS.

MY STEPFATHER DIED. HE THREW HIMSELF INTO THE SEA BECAUSE HE THOUGHT I WAS DEAD IN THE LABYRINTH.

I WANTED TO BRING HIM BACK, BUT I COULD NOT.

THE SOUL EXCHANGE. ASK HIM ABOUT THAT.

THAT VOICE. I KNOW THAT VOICE.

FOCUS. A SOUL FOR A SOUL. IS IT TRUE?

I MUST SAY... YES.

BUT BEWARE. HE IS COMING.

HE HAS SENSED YOUR SUMMONS.

PERCY? ARE YOU ALL RIGHT?

...I'M FINE. STILL SHAKING OFF LAST NIGHT'S *BAD DREAMS.*

THE LABYRINTH WAS DESIGNED TO GET INSIDE YOUR HEAD.

I DON'T LIKE THE IDEA OF ANY OF YOU GOING DOWN THERE.

IT EXISTS TO FOOL YOU. TO DISTRACT YOU.

THAT'S *DANGEROUS* FOR HALF-BLOODS.

KEEP YOUR MIND ON WHAT MATTERS MOST. IF YOU CAN DO THAT, YOU MIGHT FIND THE WAY.

HERE, I WANTED TO GIVE YOU SOMETHING.

A *DOG WHISTLE?*

IT'S...IT'S *FREEZING.*

IT'S MADE FROM *STYGIAN ICE* FROM THE RIVER STYX. VERY DELICATE. IT WON'T MELT, BUT IT'LL *SHATTER* WHEN YOU BLOW IT. SO ONLY USE IT WHEN YOU REALLY NEED HELP.

USE IT FOR WHAT?

THERE IS NO MORE TIME TO DELAY. WE WILL ERECT DEFENSES HERE AS BEST WE CAN.

BUT I NEED NOT REMIND YOU THAT IT IS MUCH MORE PREFERABLE THAT LUKE'S ATTACK *NEVER* COMES.

I OFFER ONE LAST WORD OF CAUTION: IT MAY NOT BE ONLY NAVIGATION THAT OUR ENEMIES SEEK.

THEY HAVE THE PIECES OF THE TITAN LORD KRONOS, TAKEN FROM TARTARUS ITSELF.

TO RESURRECT HIM FULLY, HE WILL NEED A *NEW FORM.*

DAEDALUS IS HISTORY'S GREATEST *INVENTOR*. HE CREATED THE LABYRINTH, BUT ALSO SO MUCH MORE. AUTOMATONS, THINKING MACHINES...

...KRONOS MAY WISH FOR DAEDALUS TO CRAFT HIM A *BODY*.

WE'LL GET TO HIM FIRST, CHIRON. OR DIE TRYING.

PRECISELY WHAT CONCERNS ME.

MAY THE GODS BE WITH YOU.

YOU READY?

AS I'LL EVER BE.

GOOD-BYE SUNSHINE.

HELLO, *ROCKS*.

WHY ARE YOU HELPING US?

I DIDN'T THINK YOU LIKED HEROES. YOU TRIED TO KILL HERCULES, LIKE, *LOTS* OF TIMES.

WATER UNDER THE BRIDGE, MY DEAR. BESIDES, HE WAS ONE OF MY LOVING HUSBAND'S CHILDREN BY *ANOTHER* WOMAN. MY PATIENCE WORE THIN.

BUT I'M THE GODDESS OF *MARRIAGE*. I'M USED TO PERSEVERANCE. YOU HAVE TO RISE ABOVE THE SQUABBLING AND CHAOS, AND KEEP BELIEVING.

AND ZEUS KNOWS I ONLY WANT TO KEEP MY FAMILY, THE OLYMPIANS, TOGETHER. HE DOESN'T ALLOW ME TO INTERFERE IN QUESTS MUCH, I'M AFRAID, BUT ON OCCASION HE ALLOWS ME TO GRANT A SINGLE WISH.

BEFORE YOU ASK IT, I'LL GIVE YOU SOME ADVICE. I KNOW YOU SEEK DAEDALUS. IF YOU WANT TO KNOW HIS FATE, I WOULD SEEK MY SON *HEPHAESTUS* AT HIS FORGE.

DAEDALUS WAS A GREAT INVENTOR. THERE HAS NEVER BEEN A MORTAL HEPHAESTUS ADMIRED MORE. IF ANYONE WOULD HAVE KEPT UP WITH DAEDALUS, IT IS HEPHAESTUS.

BUT HOW DO WE GET THERE?

THAT'S MY *WISH!*

I WANT A WAY TO *NAVIGATE* THE *LABYRINTH!*

SO BE IT. YOU WISH FOR SOMETHING, HOWEVER, THAT YOU HAVE ALREADY BEEN GIVEN.

THE MEANS ARE WITHIN YOUR GRASP.

PERCY KNOWS THE ANSWER.

...I DO?

THAT'S NOT *FAIR!* YOU'RE NOT *TELLING* US WHAT IT IS!

GETTING SOMETHING AND HAVING THE WITS TO USE IT...THOSE ARE TWO DIFFERENT THINGS. I'M SURE YOUR MOTHER *ATHENA* WOULD AGREE.

NOW, I MUST GO. ONE LAST THING, ANNABETH. SOON, YOU WILL HAVE TO MAKE A *CHOICE*. ONE BAD CHOICE CAN RUIN YOUR LIFE. IT CAN KILL YOU AND ALL YOUR FRIENDS.

WHO'S THERE? *TALK!*

THE TITANS WILL RISE AND THROW US ALL BACK INTO TARTARUS.

KAMPÊ IS BACK.

WE'RE GOING *CAMPING* NOW?

NOT "CAMPING." *KAMPÊ.* SHE WAS A JAILER FOR KRONOS.

WHEN THE TITANS RULED, SHE IMPRISONED THE CYCLOPES AND HEKATONKHEIRES-- THE HUNDRED-HANDED ONES.

LIKE *HIM*.

HEKATONKHEIRES AND CYCLOPES... FRIENDS...

BRIARES!

YOU'RE SO STRONG, YOU BREAK *MOUNTAINS!*

I AM TYSON! I WANT YOUR *AUTOGRAPH!*

"WE NEED A PLACE TO CAMP FOR THE NIGHT."

ZZZZZZ

YOU SHOULD SLEEP, TOO, PERCY.

CAN'T. YOU DOING ALL RIGHT?

SURE. FIRST DAY LEADING THE QUEST. JUST GREAT.

I WAS KIDDING MYSELF. ALL THAT PLANNING AND READING ABOUT THE LABYRINTH. I DON'T HAVE A *CLUE* WHERE WE'RE GOING.

WE NEVER HAVE A CLUE. IT ALWAYS WORKS OUT.

WHAT DID HERA MEAN WHEN SHE SAID YOU KNEW THE WAY TO GET THROUGH THE MAZE?

I DON'T KNOW. HONESTLY.

YOU WANT TO TALK ABOUT THE LAST LINE OF THE PROPHECY? OR WHAT HERA MEANT WHEN SHE SAID YOU'D HAVE TO MAKE A CHOICE?

NICO IS DOWN HERE SOMEWHERE.

HE FOUND THE LABYRINTH, THEN FOUND A PATH THAT LED DOWN EVEN FARTHER-- ALL THE WAY TO THE *UNDERWORLD.*

NOW HE'S BACK IN THE MAZE, AND HE'S COMING FOR ME.

PERCY, I HOPE YOU'RE WRONG. BECAUSE IF YOU'RE RIGHT...

YEAH.

THEY LET MY *SISTER BIANCA* DIE! SHE WENT ON A *QUEST* WITH THEM, AND SHE NEVER CAME BACK!

THEY'RE HERE TO *KILL* ME!

PUT THAT AWAY, NICO. I AIN'T GONNA HAVE MY GUESTS KILLIN' EACH OTHER.

PERCY JACKSON, ANNABETH CHASE, AND A COUPLE OF THEIR MONSTER FRIENDS. I KNOW *DARN* WELL WHO THEY ARE. I MAKE IT MY BUSINESS TO KEEP INFORMED.

BUT, GERYON, THAT'S--

NOW PUT THAT UGLY SWORD AWAY BEFORE I HAVE EURYTION TAKE IT FROM YOU.

I *HATE* STYGIAN IRON.

I'M *WARNING* YOU, PERCY.

IF YOU COME NEAR ME, I'LL SUMMON HELP.

YOU DON'T WANT TO MEET MY HELPERS, I PROMISE.

I BELIEVE YOU.

THERE, WE'VE ALL MADE NICE.

NOW COME ALONG, FOLKS.

"I GOT LUNCH ON."

TRIPLE G RANCH.

QUINTUS...

SHORT GRAY HAIR? MUSCULAR, SWORDSMAN? NEVER HEARD OF HIM.

YOUR MARK WAS ON THE CRATES AT CAMP. *QUINTUS* GOT HIS SCORPIONS FROM YOU.

WE GOT A LOT MORE THAN GIANT SCORPIONS, THOUGH. FIRE-BREATHING HORSES, HIPPALEKTRYONS. THE HERDS OF SUN COWS MAKE GREAT EATING.

YOU KNOW THE SAYING--AN *ARMY* MARCHES ON ITS STOMACH.

¿ACK¿ WHAT'S THAT *STENCH*?

POOP.

MY STABLES. WELL, ACTUALLY THEY BELONG TO AEGEAS. BUT I WATCH OVER THEM FOR A FEE. THAT'S WHERE WE KEEP THE PRIZE *FLESH-EATING* HORSES.

THEY'RE A LITTLE...MESSY. BUT WHAT DOES AN ARMY CARE?

PLUS, YOU'RE TOO *CHEAP* TO HIRE SOMEONE TO CLEAN UP AFTER THEM.

YOU SEE, NICO, *LUKE* IS OFFERING VERY GOOD MONEY FOR HALF-BLOODS. ESPECIALLY *POWERFUL* ONES.

I'M SURE WHEN HE LEARNS YOU'RE THE SON OF HADES, HE'LL PAY VERY, *VERY* WELL INDEED.

YOU *FIEND!*

AS FOR THE REST OF YOU, DON'T WORRY. I'VE BEEN PAID WELL TO GIVE YOUR QUEST SAFE PASSAGE.

WE AREN'T LEAVING WITHOUT NICO.

IF YOU'RE SMART, THAT'S *EXACTLY* WHAT YOU'LL DO.

YOU SAID YOU'RE A BUSINESSMAN, GERYON. SO LET'S MAKE A *DEAL.*

IF I CAN CLEAN YOUR STABLES, YOU LET ALL OF US GO. *INCLUDING* NICO.

IF I FAIL, YOU CAN *SELL* US ALL TO LUKE.

NO! I DON'T WANT *YOUR* HELP, PERCY!

DEAL. YOU HAVE UNTIL SUNSET. NO LATER.

NOW RUN ALONG. I'LL KEEP YOUR FRIENDS HERE WITH ME.

PERCY, I HOPE YOU KNOW WHAT YOU'RE DOING.

ME, TOO.

I CLEANED YOUR STABLES, GERYON. WE HAD A *DEAL*.

LET MY FRIENDS GO.

I'VE BEEN THINKING ABOUT THAT.

THE PROBLEM IS, IF I LET THEM GO, I DON'T GET *PAID*.

AND IN ANY EVENT, YOU DIDN'T MAKE ME SWEAR ON THE RIVER STYX.

WHEN YOU'RE CONDUCTING BUSINESS, SONNY, YOU SHOULD *ALWAYS* GET A LEGALLY BINDING OATH.

EURYTION, THIS ONE *ANNOYS* ME. KILL HIM.

NO, DON'T THINK I WILL.

EXCUSE ME?

YOU KEEP SENDING ME TO DO YOUR DIRTY WORK. YOU PICK FIGHTS FOR NO GOOD REASON. THESE HALF-BLOODS DIDN'T DO ANYTHING TO YOU.

YOU WANT TO FIGHT THE KID?

DO IT YOURSELF.

FINE!

THANKS FOR STAYING OUT OF IT, EURYTION.

SHOOT. I'VE WORKED FOR THAT CREEP FOR THOUSANDS OF YEARS.

STARTED OUT A REGULAR HALF-BLOOD, BUT I CHOSE IMMORTALITY WHEN MY DAD, *ARES*, OFFERED IT.

WORST MISTAKE I EVER MADE. NOW I'M *STUCK* HERE AT THIS RANCH.

I CAN'T LEAVE. I CAN'T QUIT. I JUST TEND THE COWS AND FIGHT GERYON'S FIGHTS. I'M FED UP WITH IT.

TIME FOR A CHANGE, DON'T YOU THINK? ONCE GERYON RE-FORMS, MAYBE *HE'LL* BE WORKING FOR *YOU.*

NOW, *THAT* I COULD LIVE WITH.

STAY HERE UNTIL WE'RE DONE WITH OUR QUEST, NICO. YOU'LL BE SAFE.

WHAT DO *YOU* CARE IF I'M SAFE? YOU GOT MY SISTER KILLED.

IF YOU *REALLY* CARED, YOU'D HELP BRING MY SISTER *BACK!*

BIANCA WOULDN'T WANT TO BE BROUGHT BACK. NOT LIKE THAT.

YOU DIDN'T KNOW HER!

HOW DO YOU KNOW WHAT SHE'D WANT?

LET'S ASK HER.

PERCY, I DON'T THINK THAT'S A GOOD--

YOU CAN SUMMON THE *DEAD*, NICO. I'VE SEEN IT IN MY DREAMS. SO LET'S ASK BIANCA WHAT SHE WANTS.

REMEMBER. YOU *ASKED* FOR THIS.

NIGHTFALL.

MMGR FRSN NGHH...

THIS ISN'T NATURAL.

MAKE HIM STOP, BROTHER.

KIRS JDOA DJH YWDE...

BIANCA, APPEAR!

WE HAVE TO CONTINUE OUR QUEST.

NICO, YOU COULD COME WITH US.

THE BOY CAN STAY HERE AND GATHER HIS THOUGHTS AS LONG AS HE WANTS. HE'LL BE SAFE, I PROMISE.

...I NEED TIME TO THINK.

I RECKON YOU'LL BE LOOKING FOR DAEDALUS'S WORKSHOP NOW? *HEPHAESTUS* COULD STEER YOU IN THE RIGHT DIRECTION.

THAT'S WHAT HERA SAID. BUT HOW DO WE FIND HIM?

I DID HEPHAESTUS A FAVOR ONCE.

A LITTLE *TRICK* HE WANTED TO PLAY ON MY DAD AND APHRODITE.

HE GAVE ME THIS DISK AS GRATITUDE.

SAID IF I EVER NEEDED TO FIND HIM, THE DISK WOULD LEAD ME TO HIM. BUT ONLY ONCE.

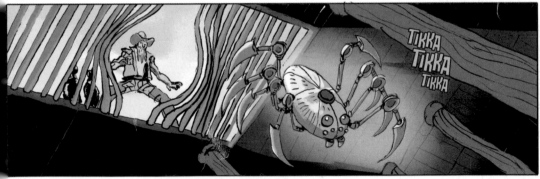

TIKKA TIKKA TIKKA

WELL? IT AIN'T GONNA *WAIT* FOR YOU.

YOU AREN'T SOME OF MY AUTOMATONS, ARE YOU?

UM. NO, SIR, MR. HEPHAESTUS.

GOOD. SHODDY WORKMANSHIP.

AT LEAST THERE'S A *CYCLOPS*. YOU GOOD WITH YOUR HANDS?

WHAT'RE YOU DOING TRAVELING WITH THIS LOT?

UH...

≹HMPH≹ THERE'D BETTER BE A GOOD REASON FOR *DISTURBING* ME.

IF YOU HAVEN'T NOTICED, I HAVE A LOT OF WORK TO DO.

SIR, WE'RE LOOKING FOR DAEDALUS. WE THOUGHT--

DAEDALUS? YOU WANT THAT OLD SCOUNDREL?

WASTE OF TIME. HE WON'T HELP YOU WITH YOUR LITTLE QUEST.

HERA SAID YOU WOULD HELP US?

DID SHE NOW? GIVE YOU A BUNCH OF TALK ABOUT *FAMILIES*, DID SHE?

THE TRUTH IS, MY MOTHER LIKES FAMILIES, BUT ONLY A CERTAIN KIND OF FAMILY. *PERFECT* FAMILIES.

I DON'T EXACTLY FIT THAT IMAGE, EH?

ASK ME FOR GOLD. OR A FLAMING SWORD. OR A MAGICAL CHARIOT. THESE I CAN GRANT YOU EASILY.

BUT A WAY TO DAEDALUS? THAT'S AN *EXPENSIVE* FAVOR.

NAME YOUR PRICE.

BAH!

YOU HEROES! ALWAYS MAKING *RASH* PROMISES!

VERY WELL. I HAVE A FAVORITE FORGE INSIDE MOUNT ST. HELENS. LATELY, I CAN TELL SOMEONE IS USING IT WITHOUT MY PERMISSION. SOMEONE *ANCIENT* AND *EVIL*.

FIND OUT WHO IS *TRESPASSING* ON MY TERRITORY AND REPORT BACK TO ME.

MY CREATION WILL SHOW YOU THE WAY. IT'S NOT FAR THROUGH THE LABYRINTH.

NOW, BEGONE. LEAVE ME TO MY WORK.

TIKKA

TIKKA

I *HAVE* TO.

I WILL GO WITH GOAT BOY.

TYSON? ARE YOU *SURE*?

I WILL HELP HIM.

I HOPE YOU'RE RIGHT.

I *KNOW* I AM!

TYSON! *LET'S GO!*

PERCY, GROVER HAS HIS OWN QUEST TO FULFILL. AND WE HAVE OURS.

I CAN FEEL THE HEAT COMING DOWN THE PASSAGEWAY.

THE FORGE IS *CLOSE*. WE CAN'T LET THE SPIDER GET AWAY.

IT'S JUST AHEAD...

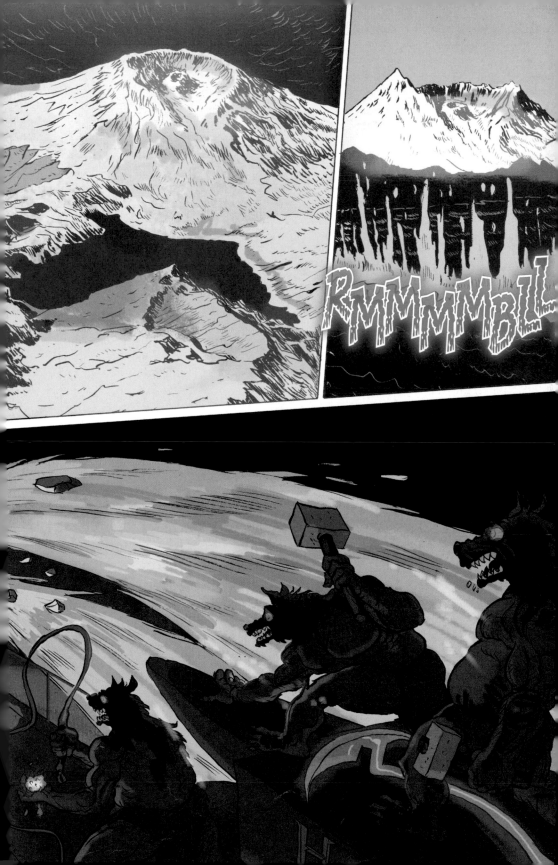

BWOOOOSH

UHNNN

HEPHAESTUS? WHAT HAPPENED? IS *ANNABETH*--

SHE'S FINE. *RESOURCEFUL* GIRL, THAT ONE. FOUND HER WAY BACK, TOLD ME THE WHOLE STORY.

SHE'S WORRIED SICK, YOU KNOW. EVERYONE SUSPECTS YOU'RE DEAD.

I KNOW *BETTER*, OF COURSE, BUT I WANTED TO BE SURE YOU WERE COMING BACK BEFORE I TOLD THEM.

COME BACK FROM *WHERE*?

WHAT IS THIS PLACE?

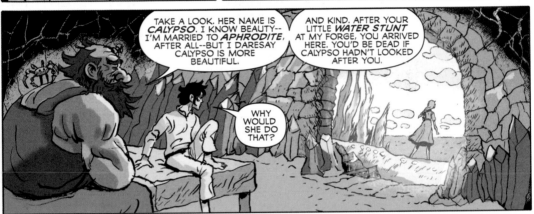

TAKE A LOOK. HER NAME IS *CALYPSO*. I KNOW BEAUTY-- I'M MARRIED TO *APHRODITE*, AFTER ALL--BUT I DARESAY CALYPSO IS MORE BEAUTIFUL.

AND KIND. AFTER YOUR LITTLE *WATER STUNT* AT MY FORGE, YOU ARRIVED HERE. YOU'D BE DEAD IF CALYPSO HADN'T LOOKED AFTER YOU.

WHY WOULD SHE DO THAT?

BECAUSE SHE MUST REMAIN IN THIS PARADISE FOREVER. *ALONE.*

UNLESS SOMEONE CHOOSES TO REMAIN WITH HER.

YOU COULD BE THAT SOMEONE. YOU'D BE SAFE HERE. FREE FROM PAIN AND WANT. A TRUE HERO'S REWARD. THERE ARE MANY *WORSE* WAYS TO SPEND ETERNITY.

LEAVE THE MORTAL WORLD TO THE MORTALS.

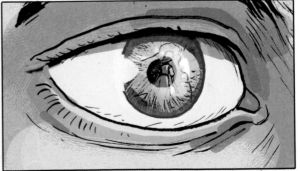

BUT IF YOU DECIDE TO LEAVE-- AND I DON'T SAY WHAT'S *RIGHT* OR *WRONG*--THEN I PROMISED YOU THE WAY TO DAEDALUS.

HERE'S THE THING. IT HAS NOTHING TO DO WITH *ARIADNE'S STRING.* SURE, THE STRING WORKS. THAT'S WHY THE TITANS' ARMY IS AFTER IT. BUT IT ISN'T THE BEST WAY THROUGH THE MAZE.

THESEUS HAD THE PRINCESS'S HELP, AND THE PRINCESS WAS A REGULAR MORTAL. BUT SHE WAS CLEVER. SHE COULD *SEE,* LAD.

SHE COULD SEE *VERY CLEARLY.* SO WHAT I'M SAYING IS, YOU ALREADY KNOW HOW TO NAVIGATE THE MAZE.

I DON'T...

I CAN'T BELIEVE I DIDN'T FIGURE IT OUT!

SEND ME BACK!

DON'T YOU AT LEAST WANT TO TALK TO CALYPSO FIRST? NO HARM IN WEIGHING YOUR OPTIONS.

SOMETHING TELLS ME IF I SEE HER...

...I WON'T WANT TO LEAVE.

WILL YOU TELL HER I SAID THANK YOU? AND I'M SORRY I CAN'T STAY?

I SUPPOSE IT WON'T BE TOO MUCH TROUBLE.

RUN ALONG NOW. TIME WORKS DIFFERENTLY HERE, LAD. YOU'VE ALREADY BEEN GONE *TOO LONG.* I LEFT A BOAT FOR YOU BY THE SHORE.

WE CAN ONLY ASSUME HE IS DEAD. AFTER SO LONG A *SILENCE*, IT IS UNLIKELY OUR PRAYERS WILL BE ANSWERED.

I HAVE ASKED HIS BEST SURVIVING FRIEND TO DO THE *FINAL HONORS* AND BURN PERCY JACKSON'S SHROUD.

HE WAS PROBABLY THE BRAVEST FRIEND I'VE EVER HAD.

HE...

HEY.

HE'S *RIGHT THERE!*

WE THOUGHT YOU WERE *DEAD*, SEAWEED BRAIN!

I'M SORRY. I GOT LOST.

I DON'T BELIEVE I'VE EVER BEEN *HAPPIER* TO SEE A CAMPER RETURN.

"BUT PERHAPS WE SHOULD DISCUSS YOUR TRIALS SOMEWHERE MORE *PRIVATE*."

YOU WERE GONE TWO WEEKS, PERCY.

TWO WEEKS?!

WHEN I HEARD THE *EXPLOSION* AT THE FORGE, I THOUGHT...

I KNOW. BUT I TALKED TO HEPHAESTUS. I FIGURED OUT HOW TO GET THROUGH THE LABYRINTH.

HE TOLD YOU THE ANSWER?

WELL, HE SORT OF TOLD ME WHAT I ALREADY KNEW. I UNDERSTAND NOW. WE NEED A *MORTAL'S* HELP.

PERCY, THAT'S *CRAZY*!

THERE IS PRECEDENT. THESEUS HAD THE HELP OF ARIADNE. *HARRIET TUBMAN*, DAUGHTER OF HERMES, USED MANY MORTALS IN HER UNDERGROUND RAILROAD.

BUT THIS IS *MY* QUEST. I NEED TO LEAD IT.

ASKING A MORTAL FOR HELP IS *WRONG*. IT'S *COWARDLY*. IT'S--

IT'S HARD TO *ADMIT* YOU NEED A MORTAL'S HELP. BUT IT'S TRUE.

YOU ARE THE *SINGLE MOST ANNOYING* PERSON I HAVE EVER MET!

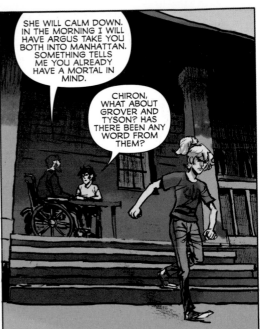

SHE WILL CALM DOWN. IN THE MORNING I WILL HAVE ARGUS TAKE YOU BOTH INTO MANHATTAN. SOMETHING TELLS ME YOU ALREADY HAVE A MORTAL IN MIND.

CHIRON, WHAT ABOUT GROVER AND TYSON? HAS THERE BEEN ANY WORD FROM THEM?

I'M AFRAID NOT.

THE COUNCIL OF CLOVEN ELDERS HAS REVOKED GROVER'S SEARCHER'S LICENSE IN ABSENTIA.

IF HE RETURNS, THEY WILL FORCE HIM INTO A *SHAMEFUL* EXILE.

AND THERE IS MORE BAD NEWS: *QUINTUS* HAS DISAPPEARED.

THREE NIGHTS AGO, HE WAS SEEN SLIPPING INTO THE LABYRINTH.

HE'S A SPY FOR LUKE. HE BOUGHT HIS SCORPIONS FROM THE TRIPLE G RANCH, THE SAME PLACE THAT'S SUPPLYING LUKE'S ARMY WITH MONSTERS.

THAT *CAN'T* BE A COINCIDENCE.

SO MANY BETRAYALS. I HAD HOPED QUINTUS WOULD PROVE HIMSELF A FRIEND. IT SEEMS MY JUDGMENT WAS BAD.

BUT WE CANNOT BE DETERRED. PREPARE FOR TOMORROW MORNING. YOU AND ANNABETH STILL HAVE *MUCH* TO DO.

MORNING.

YOU LOOK BEAT. BAD DREAMS?

A MESSAGE FROM *EURYTION.* NICO LEFT THE RANCH LAST NIGHT. HE HEADED BACK INTO THE MAZE.

WHAT? EURYTION DIDN'T TRY TO STOP HIM?

NICO WAS GONE BEFORE HE WOKE UP. HE SAID HE'D HEARD NICO TALKING TO HIMSELF THE LAST COUPLE OF NIGHTS.

ONLY NOW HE THINKS NICO WAS TALKING TO THE GHOST AGAIN. *MINOS.*

NICO IS IN DANGER. I HAD THIS DREAM LAST NIGHT... I SAW *LUKE* IN THE LABYRINTH. THEY FOUND A HALF-BLOOD WANDERING ALONE.

THIS IS VERY, *VERY* BAD.

THEN IT'S A GOOD THING YOU HAVE A PLAN TO *GUIDE* US, SEAWEED BRAIN.

TIMES SQUARE.

THIS IS WHO YOU'RE TRUSTING THE FATE OF THE WORLD TO?

SHE'S AN ARTIST. THIS MUST BE SOME KIND OF PERFORMANCE ART.

RIGHT?

GOOD TIMING, PERCY. YOU CAUGHT ME GOING INTO BREAK.

MY CLASS IS DOING AN ART PROJECT TO RAISE MONEY FOR ELEMENTARY SCHOOL ART PROGRAMS.

YOU WERE PRETTY *VAGUE* ON THE PHONE. WHAT'S UP?

MY FRIEND ANNABETH AND I HAVE A PROBLEM.

PERCY THINKS WE NEED YOUR HELP. I'M NOT CONVINCED.

HELP? SURE. *NO PROBLEM.* EVERY TIME I'M AROUND YOU, *MONSTERS* ATTACK US. NOT TO MENTION, SCHOOL STILL WANTS ME TO EXPLAIN HOW THE BAND ROOM MYSTERIOUSLY *BLEW UP.*

I'M WITH ANNABELLE. I CAN'T SEE HOW I'D BE MUCH HELP.

ANNA*BETH.*

YOU CAN SEE THROUGH THE *MIST.* YOU KNEW THOSE COPS WEREN'T REALLY COPS AT THE HOOVER DAM. AND YOU KNEW THOSE GIRLS WEREN'T REALLY CHEERLEADERS.

I THINK YOU CAN *GUIDE* US.

GUIDE YOU? *WHERE?*

TELL HER, ANNABETH.

TELL HER.

FINE!

WE'RE TRYING TO NAVIGATE THE LABYRINTH FROM ANCIENT GREEK MYTH. IF YOU CAN SEE THROUGH MIST, THERE'S A CHANCE IT WON'T CONFUSE YOU AS MUCH AS IT DOES US.

BUT FIRST WE NEED TO GET YOU INSIDE. HAVE YOU SEEN ANY ENTRANCES? THEY'D HAVE THE MARK OF DAEDALUS. IT'S LIKE A GLOWING BLUE TRIANGLE.

HAVE YOU SEEN ANY? NO? GREAT.

LET'S GO, PERCY. SHE'S *USELESS.*

RACHEL?

DID YOU SAY A *BLUE TRIANGLE?*

IS THIS WHAT YOU'RE LOOKING FOR?

WE STORE OUR COSTUMES FOR THE ART PROJECTS IN THIS ROOM. NO ONE ELSE HAS NOTICED THE SYMBOL, SO I FIGURED IT WAS ME GOING *CRAZY* AGAIN. I'VE TOUCHED IT, BUT NOTHING HAPPENS.

THAT'S BECAUSE YOU'RE *MORTAL*. IT NEEDS THE TOUCH OF A HALF-BLOOD.

CREEEEEAK

RIGHT. A *LABYRINTH*, YOU SAID?

AFTER YOU.

YOU'RE SUPPOSED TO BE THE GUIDE. LEAD ON.

BAH! THIS *ENTERTAINMENT* IS NOTHING I HAVEN'T SEEN BEFORE!

WHAT ELSE DO YOU HAVE, *LUKE*, SON OF *HERMES*?

LORD ANTAEUS, YOU HAVE BEEN AN EXCELLENT HOST. WE WOULD BE HAPPY TO AMUSE YOU, TO EARN YOUR FAVOR AND *SAFE PASSAGE* THROUGH YOUR TERRITORY.

WAIT, ANTAEUS. MY *MINION* HAS SOMETHING TO TELL ME.

I HAVE SOMETHING *FAR BETTER* THAN CENTAURS TO FIGHT IN YOUR ARENA. I PRESENT A *BROTHER* OF YOURS, A FELLOW *SON OF POSEIDON*--

--PERCY JACKSON!

DEATH!

LET'S EAT HIM!

A SON OF POSEIDON? THEN HE SHOULD FIGHT WELL! OR *DIE* WELL!

YOU WILL ALL SEE WHY I AM POSEIDON'S *FAVORITE* SON! HERE, IN THE TEMPLE OF THE *EARTHSHAKER*, ADORNED WITH THE *SKULLS* OF ALL THOSE I'VE KILLED IN HIS NAME!

GUYS, THE PATH WE NEED TO FOLLOW...
...WE HAVE TO GO THROUGH THE ARENA TO GET TO IT.
PLAYING HOST TO LUKE, ANTAEUS? I DON'T THINK DAD WOULD LIKE THAT VERY MUCH.
WANT TO FIND OUT WHO THE FAVORITE SON IS? WINNER TAKE ALL. YOU AND ME.
IF I BEAT YOU, YOU LET US PASS. YOU WIN, YOU GET TO KILL US.
PERCY! DON'T!
WHOOOM
KRAKAKK
THIS SHOULDN'T TAKE LONG. I'M THE WORLD'S GREATEST WRESTLER, BOY. AND WHEN I STARTED, THERE WAS NONE OF THIS ONE-TWO-THREE-COUNT STUFF.
WE WRESTLED UNTIL SOMEONE DIED.

YOUR *MOM* CAN'T HELP YOU IF YOU AREN'T *TOUCHING THE GROUND!*
OOP.
FOOOOMP!

IF YOU GUYS ARE WAITING FOR *ME* TO SEE A WAY OUT OF THIS, DON'T.

PERCY? ANY IDEAS?

I...

WHAT'S THERE TO LOSE?

FWEEEEEEEEET

WHAT, *EXACTLY*, DID YOU THINK THAT WAS GOING TO ACCOMPLISH?

SO I GAVE IT TO HIM. AND IN RETURN, KRONOS PROMISED ME THAT ONCE HADES IS OVERTHROWN, HE WILL SET ME OVER THE UNDERWORLD.

YOU SEE, I HAVE MY OWN PAST TO MAKE GOOD FOR. A MAN CAN MAKE A LOT OF MISTAKES IN TWO THOUSAND YEARS. THIS IS THE ONLY WAY I CAN BE SURE I DON'T SUFFER FOR THEM.

THAT'S YOUR BRILLIANT IDEA? TO LET LUKE DESTROY CAMP, KILL ALL THE DEMIGODS, AND THEN ATTACK OLYMPUS?

TO LET KRONOS BRING DOWN THE ENTIRE WORLD TO GET WHAT YOU WANT?

IF YOU HAD A CHANCE, I MIGHT HELP YOU. BUT YOUR CAUSE IS DOOMED, MY DEAR. THERE IS NO WAY YOU CAN HOLD BACK THE MIGHT OF THE TITAN LORD.

WELL SAID, OLD MAN.

LUKE'S MINIONS?

WHAT IS THE MEANING OF THIS? THIS WAS NOT OUR ARRANGEMENT.

THERE'S A NEW ARRANGEMENT. YOUR OLD EMPLOYER, MINOS, WANTED TO SEE YOU. AND HE TRADED A MOST INTERESTING DEMIGOD FOR THE PRIVILEGE.

A CHILD OF HADES. KRONOS WILL HAVE MANY USES FOR THIS ONE.

AND I WILL RULE OVER THE AFTERLIFE, DAEDALUS. I LOOK FORWARD TO SEEING YOU THERE.

CAMP. WE HAVE TO GET BACK THERE AND WARN THEM THAT LUKE HAS ARIADNE'S STRING.

IT WON'T BE LONG BEFORE THE *TITAN ARMY* INVADES.

IF THEY HAVEN'T INVADED ALREADY.

RACHEL, THE FASTEST WAY BACK TO CAMP IS THROUGH THE LABYRINTH.

CAN YOU FIND US ANOTHER ENTRANCE?

THERE.

THAT ABANDONED MINESHAFT.

IT'S LIT UP LIKE A *FREEWAY.*

THAT WAY.

HIDE THE WINGS, SO NO ONE FINDS THEM.

THERE'S SOMETHING ON THE GROUND. IS THAT...

GROVER'S HAT!

PERCY...

"LET'S GO HOME."

MANHATTAN.

THANKS, RACHEL. WE COULDN'T HAVE DONE ANY OF THIS WITHOUT YOU. SORRY YOU CAN'T COME WITH US, BUT MORTALS AT CAMP ARE A BIG *NO-NO*.

IT'S DEFINITELY BEEN A...*UNIQUE* EXPERIENCE.

IF YOU EVER FEEL LIKE HANGING OUT WITH A MORTAL AGAIN, YOU COULD CALL ME OR SOMETHING.

UH, YEAH. SURE.

I MEAN... I'D LIKE THAT.

AHEM.

TIME TO GO.

YOU GUYS NEED ME TO CALL YOU A RIDE? MY DAD HAS A CAR SERVICE.

THANKS, BUT NO NEED.

I ALREADY ARRANGED TRANSPORTATION.

WAPP

YOU DARED TO RELEASE MY PRISONER, BRIARES!

YOU WILL BE PUNISHED!

THIS COULD BE IT.

NICE FIGHTING WITH YOU, SEAWEED BRAIN.

KRONOS MIGHT PREFER TO FLAY YOU HIMSELF--

--BUT I'VE EARNED THE PRIVILEGE!

BRIARES! I *KNEW* YOU WOULD COME!

I FOUND HIM WANDERING THE LABYRINTH. FIGURED I'D BRING HIM HERE TO JOIN THE FIGHT.

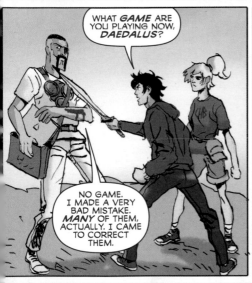

WHAT *GAME* ARE YOU PLAYING NOW, *DAEDALUS*?

NO GAME. I MADE A VERY BAD MISTAKE. *MANY* OF THEM, ACTUALLY. I CAME TO CORRECT THEM.

ANNABETH, A GIFT. IT IS ALL I COULD SALVAGE FROM THE FIRE IN MY WORKSHOP. IT HAS ALL OF MY NOTES. SOME OF MY FAVORITE DESIGNS THAT I COULD NOT BUILD OVER THE YEARS.

NOW IT IS TIME FOR MY MOST *NOTORIOUS* CREATION TO END. THE LABYRINTH IS TIED TO MY LIFE FORCE. WHEN I DIE, SO WILL IT.

YOU MEAN...

I MEAN *GENIUS* DOES NOT EXCUSE WRONGDOING.

AND IT IS WRONG TO HIDE FROM DEATH FOR SO MANY YEARS.

I OFFER YOU MY SOUL AS RANSOM, SON OF HADES. YOU CAN RECLAIM YOUR SISTER.

NO. I WILL HELP YOU RELEASE YOUR SPIRIT.

BUT BIANCA HAS PASSED. SHE MUST STAY WHERE SHE IS.

SUMMER NEARS ITS END.

DID YOU HEAR ABOUT GROVER? THE COUNCIL OF CLOVEN ELDERS DIDN'T BELIEVE HIS STORY ABOUT PAN, SO MR. D *DISSOLVED* IT. GROVER IS LEADING THE SATYRS NOW.

IF THERE'S ANYONE READY TO PROTECT THE LAST WILD PLACES, IT'S HIM.

BRIARES WENT TO HELP POSEIDON MAKE WEAPONS IN THE UNDERSEA FORGES.

TYSON IS STAYING TO HELP AT CAMP.

THAT'S EVERYTHING THEN. THE QUEST DIDN'T GO THE WAY I PLANNED, BUT AT LEAST WE WON THE BATTLE OF THE LABYRINTH.

IT'S NOT QUITE EVERYTHING.

"DESTROY WITH A HERO'S FINAL BREATH." THE SECOND-TO-LAST LINE OF THE PROPHECY MAKES SENSE NOW. DAEDALUS HAD TO DIE TO DESTROY THE MAZE.

BUT YOU NEVER SAID WHAT THE *LAST* LINE WAS.

"AND LOSE A LOVE TO WORSE THAN DEATH."

THAT WAS THE LAST LINE, PERCY. ARE YOU HAPPY NOW?

OH. SO...

I'VE BEEN THINKING ABOUT IT ALL SUMMER, AND I STILL DON'T KNOW WHO THE LAST LINE WAS TALKING ABOUT. I DON'T KNOW IF...

LUKE AND I...FOR YEARS, HE WAS THE ONLY ONE WHO REALLY CARED ABOUT ME.

I FIGURED WE'D FACE HIM AT THE BATTLE, BUT NOW I DON'T KNOW WHAT'S HAPPENED TO HIM...

RIGHT. *LUKE.*

PERCY, I DON'T MEAN IT LIKE THAT.

I DON'T KNOW *WHAT* I MEAN.

WE HAVE *OTHER* PROBLEMS RIGHT NOW.

NICO?

I'VE DONE SOME EXPLORING IN THE *UNDERWORLD.* I'VE FOUND OUT SOME THINGS.

I'M HERE TO MAKE YOU AN *OFFER.*

WHAT OFFER?

A WAY TO BEAT KRONOS. IF I'M RIGHT, IT'S THE *ONLY* WAY.

AND IT STARTS IN THE REALM OF THE *DEAD.*